HOW DID THAT GET TO MY HOUSE? HOW DID THAT GET TO MY HOUSE? HOW DID THAT GET TO MY HOUSE? HOW DID THAT GET TO MY HOUSE?

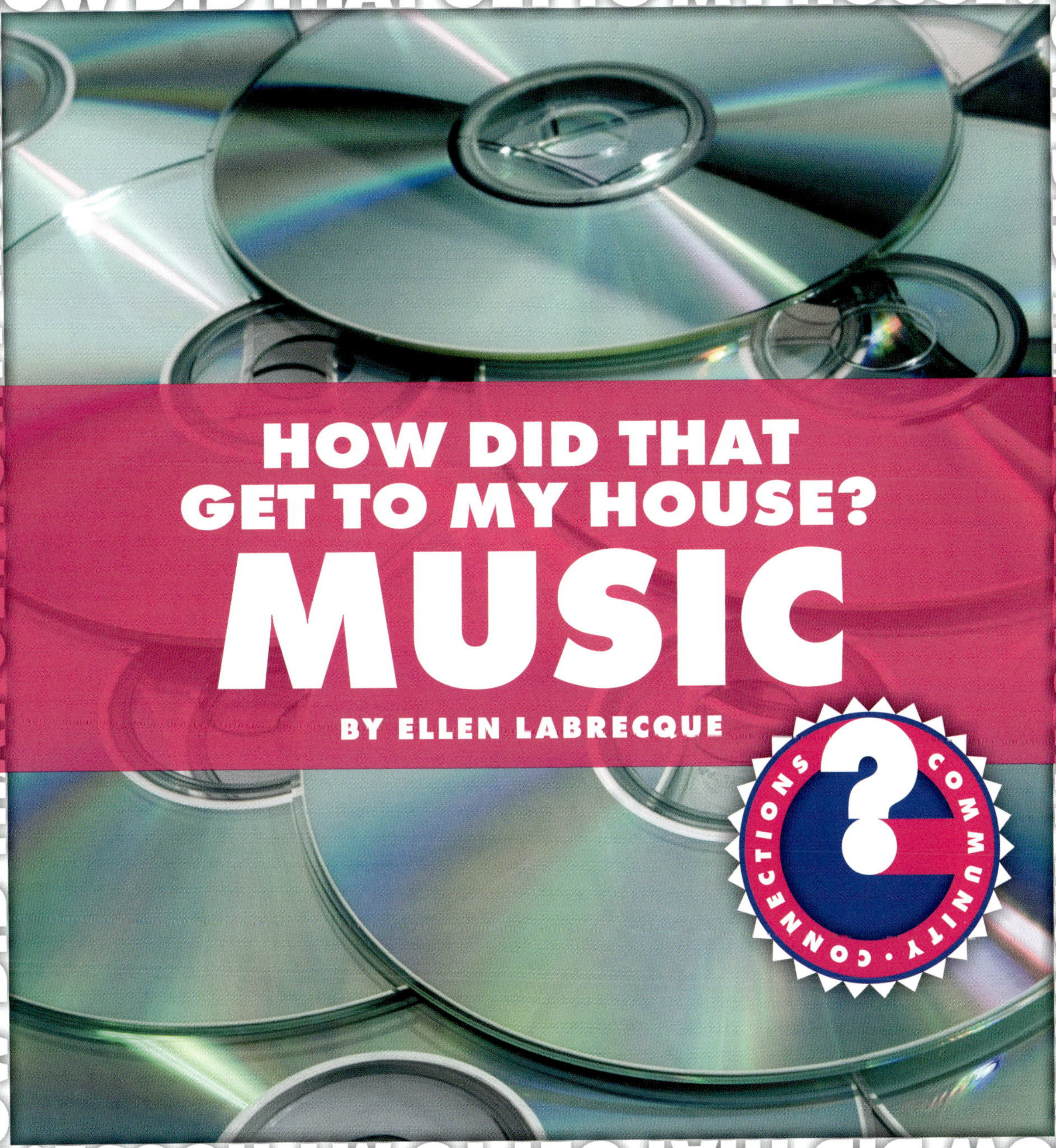

HOW DID THAT GET TO MY HOUSE?
MUSIC

BY ELLEN LABRECQUE

COMMUNITY CONNECTIONS

Published in the United States of America by Cherry Lake Publishing
Ann Arbor, Michigan
www.cherrylakepublishing.com

Content Adviser: Carlos Abril, PhD, Assistant Professor, Northwestern University, Evanston, Illinois
Reading Adviser: Cecilia Minden-Cupp, PhD, Literacy Consultant

Photo Credits: Cover and page 1, ©2happy, used under license from Shutterstock, Inc.; page 5, ©Vladimir Mucibabic, used under license from Shutterstock, Inc.; page 7, ©Gelpi, used under license from Shutterstock, Inc.; page 9, ©ICP/Alamy; page 11, ©Yanstav/Dreamstime.com; page 13, ©Anikasalsera/Dreamstime.com; page 15, ©AP Photo/Sara D. Davis; page 17, ©Stocksearch/Alamy; page 19, ©Sudheersakthan/Dreamstime.com; page 21, ©JHDT Stock Images LLC, used under license from Shutterstock, Inc.

LIBRARY OF CONGRESS CATALOGING-IN-PUBLICATION DATA
Labrecque, Ellen.
How did that get to my house? Music / by Ellen Labrecque.
p. cm.—(Community connections)
Includes index.
ISBN-13: 978-1-60279-481-8
ISBN-10: 1-60279-481-2
1. Music appreciation—Juvenile literature. I. Title. II. Series.
ML3928.L33 2010
780—dc22 2008047941

Cherry Lake Publishing would like to acknowledge the work of The Partnership for 21st Century Skills. Please visit *www.21stcenturyskills.org* for more information.

CONTENTS

WHAT IS MUSIC?

Do you like to dance and sing along to music? Have you ever wondered how that music gets to your house? How did that tune arrive on your computer? How did that song end up on your radio? Let's learn about music's journey to your home.

Listening to music is fun!

Music is the art of sound. Good music is like a beautiful painting. It takes many strokes to paint a picture. It takes many hours to create a great song. The tune of a song is called the melody. The words are the lyrics. Together, they make up a song.

Some people like to make their own music.

LOOK!

Music is all around you. How many times in one day did you hear music? Did you hear it on your television? Did you hear it in a store? Do you make music yourself?

HOW IS A SONG MADE?

A song starts as an idea. A **musician** writes the lyrics and a melody. Then the musician **records** the song.

Many musicians use a piano to write their songs.

ASK QUESTIONS!

Some musicians write the lyrics to a song first. Others write the melody first. Do you know any musicians? Ask them how they write their songs. Do they write the lyrics and melody at the same time? Find out what works for them.

Musicians record music in a studio. A studio is a special room used to record music. Studios are soundproof. That means outside noises can't be heard inside. This helps the music sound clear. It might take musicians many tries to get the song just right.

Musicians use many tools to record music. The tools help make the music sound good.

What happens when the musician thinks the song is just right? A master **CD** of the song is made. Then the master CD is sent to a factory. The factory makes many copies of the CD. Now the song is ready for a release date. That is when you can buy the CD and bring it home.

A master CD is the first step in getting music into stores.

LISTEN UP!

Copies of the CDs go to stores around the country. Stores start selling the CDs on the release date. Then you can buy the CD. You can put it in your CD player and listen to the music.

Music stores have many different kinds of music to choose from.

MOTHERSHIP
5
BURIAL

Music is also sold **electronically**. This means a song can be found at an **online** store. One popular online music store is iTunes. You can buy songs there. You **download** the songs to your computer. Then you can play the music through your computer. You can also put the music on an iPod or other music player.

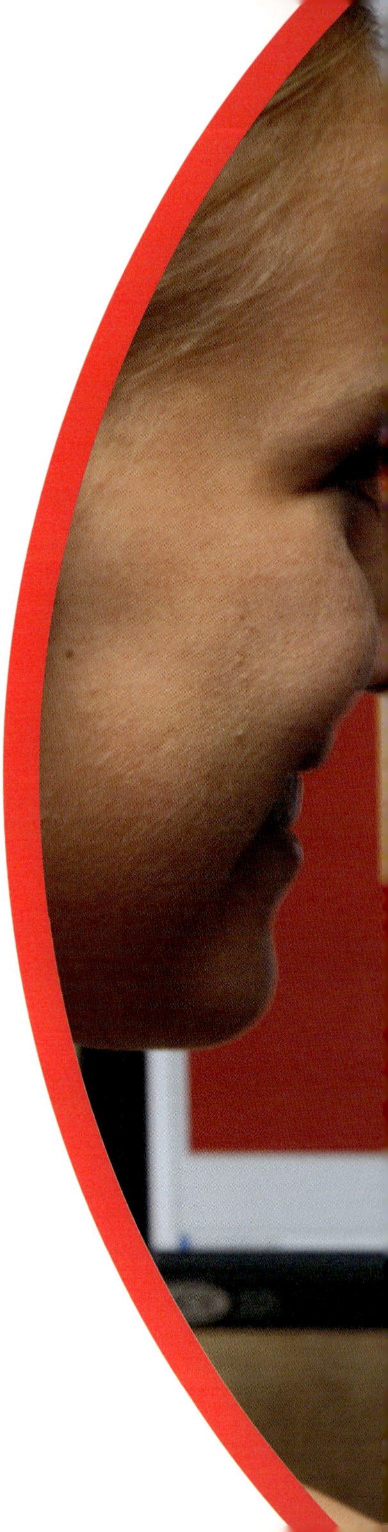

You can often listen to samples of music at online stores. Then you can decide if you want to download some songs.

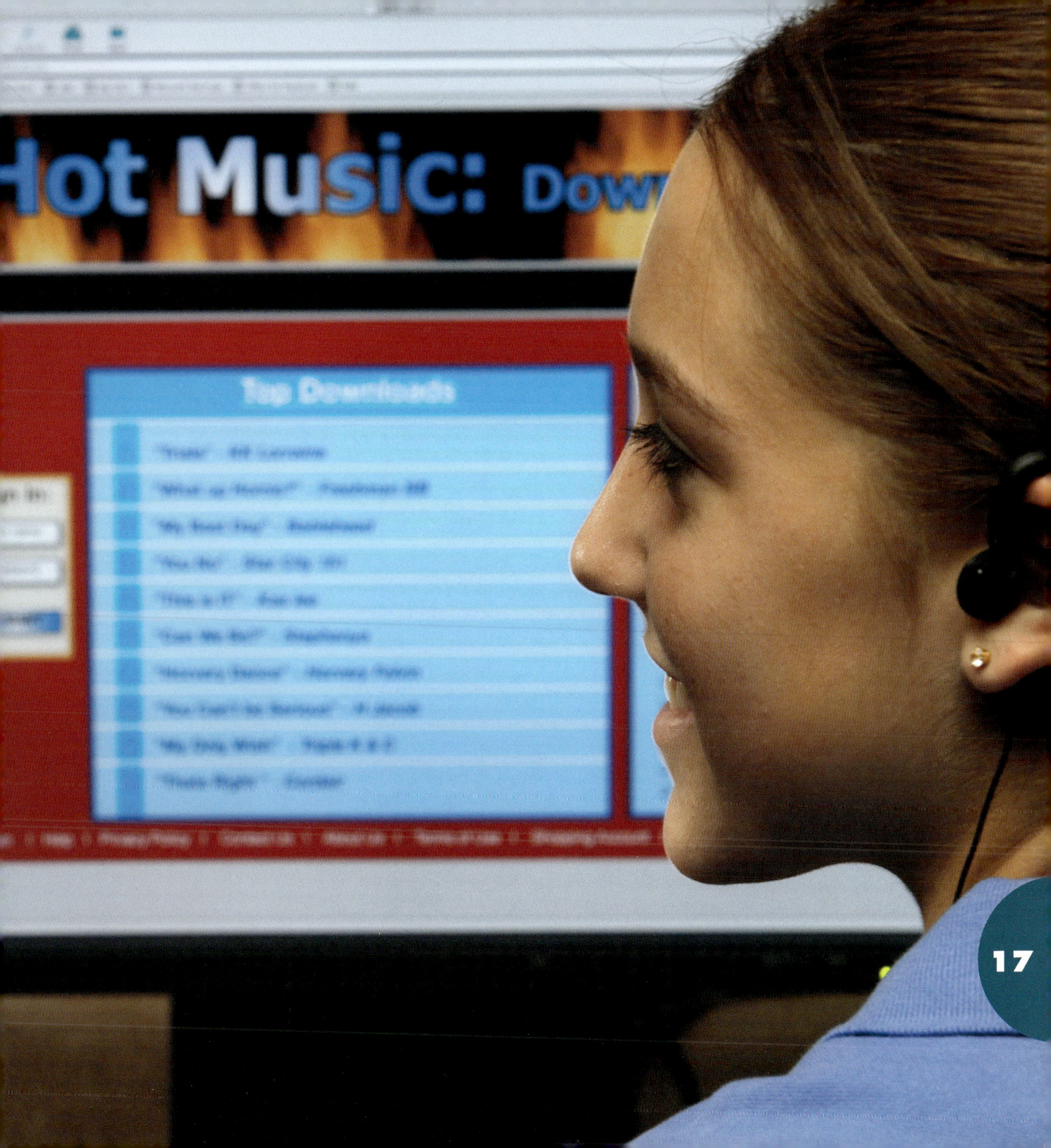
Hot Music:
Top Downloads

Radio stations also play the music. **Radio waves** carry the music over the air. The radios in our homes receive the radio waves. That is another way to hear music at home!

You can also listen to music on the radio in your car.

CREATE!

Why don't you try writing a song? You can write about anything. Your song can be about your best friend. It can be about your school. You could even write a song about ice cream! Put the words to a simple melody. How does it sound when you sing it?

Now you know how music gets to your house. Buy a CD, download a song, or turn on your radio. Music's journey to your home is finally complete. Now you can enjoy your favorite tunes!

Turn on some music and enjoy!

GLOSSARY

CD (see-DEE) a small disc that holds recorded music

download (DOWN-lohd) to transfer information from a computer system to a disk or to the memory of another computer

electronically (ee-lek-TRON-ik-lee) done with the use of a computer

musician (MYOO-zish-uhn) a person who composes or performs music

online (ON-line) connected to or available from a group of computers

radio waves (RAY-dee-oh WAYVZ) something that is made when electricity is passed through a magnet; radio waves can't be seen but can carry sound through the air

records (ri-KORDZ) puts music on a tape or disk so it can be played back and reproduced

FIND OUT MORE

BOOKS

Ardley, Neil, and Poul Ruders. *A Young Person's Guide to Music.* New York: Dorling Kindersley Publishing Inc., 2005.

Buckley, Annie. *Music.* Ann Arbor, MI: Cherry Lake Publishing, 2009.

WEB SITES

Morton Subotnick's Creating Music

www.creatingmusic.com
Visit this site to learn how to create your own music

NASA: The Electromagnetic Spectrum—Radio Waves

science.hq.nasa.gov/kids/imagers/ems/radio.html
Learn more about radio waves

INDEX

ABOUT THE AUTHOR

Ellen Labrecque is a freelance writer living in New Jersey. She has written many children's books. She would like to thank musicians Bill McGarvey and Josh Max for their help with this book. Their music is available on iTunes! Bill records using his own name, and Josh is part of a group called The Maxes.